MORE THAN ASHES

A SUSSEX CRIME NOVELLA

By Isabella Muir

Published in Great Britain
By Outset Publishing Ltd

Published February 2019

ISBN:1-872889-19-0

ISBN:978-1-872889-19-1

www.isabellamuir.com

Cover photo: by Alissa Eady on Unsplash
Cover design: by Christoffer Petersen
Map of Tamarisk Bay: by Richard Whincop

'Our greatest glory is not in never falling, but in rising
every time we fall.'
Oliver Goldsmith 1730-1774

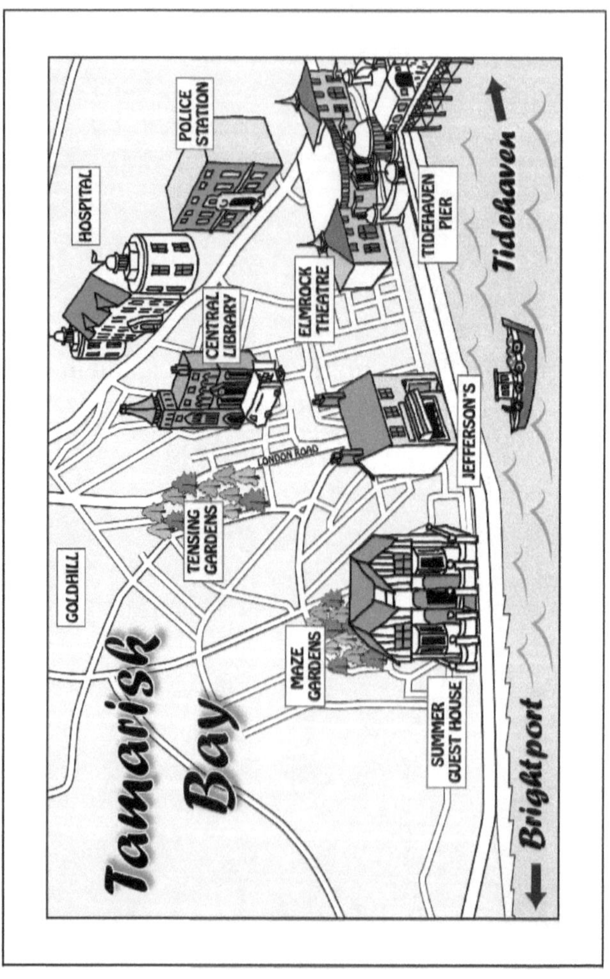

Tamarisk Bay
GOLDHILL
HOSPITAL
POLICE STATION
CENTRAL LIBRARY
ELMROCK THEATRE
TIDEHAVEN PIER
Tidehaven
TENSING GARDENS
LONDON ROAD
JEFFERSON'S
MAZE GARDENS
SUMMER GUEST HOUSE
Brightport

1
Thursday, 5th September 1940

Achieving any kind of transformation requires not just skill, but a great deal of patience and determination. Freda had the skill and plenty of determination, but not always the patience. Although Phyllis's companionship made all the difference.

Curtains that may have been a little ragged around the hems could be trimmed and restitched to make a shirt or blouse. The blackout meant flimsy cotton curtains just wouldn't do. But a flimsy cotton blouse for a child who had arrived with nothing, bar the clothes she stood up in, would do very nicely indeed.

Freda shifted the pile of material from the seat beside her so that Phyllis could sit.

'I've brought my sewing basket, there's a good selection of colours, but we won't always be able to match the stitching.'

'There's no-one going to be looking at the colour of thread, I can assure you of that,' Freda said.

'Another trainful headed off yesterday?'

'The youngest just four years old, clinging to her brother's hand as though her life depended on it; which I suppose it does in a way.'

Phyllis picked a piece of net curtain from one of the piles. 'This will make a nice collar or two and if I cut it just here and trim it I might even stretch it to several.' Her focus was on the netting for a moment or two and then, 'The town will soon be empty. One minute they're being evacuated here for safety, the next they discover this is the least safe place for them to be. All because of the relentless bombing.'

At that moment the air-raid siren sounded. It was as if the Germans were listening to the conversation between the two friends.

'Leave everything as it is. Hopefully it'll be still there when we get back.'

Phyllis followed her friend into the hallway and watched as she unlatched the door to the understairs cupboard. She'd been down into Freda's basement once before, just three nights earlier, when the previous bombing raid had taken out three houses in the neighbouring street, along with the Scouts hut. Some of the debris was still to be cleared and now it was happening again.

'I'm not sure where I feel worse.' Freda slid some of the coats to one side, revealing the trapdoor leading down to the basement. 'This blessed shoe rack is always in the way. Every time I come in here I promise I'll move it and then it just goes clear out of my head.' She pushed the shoe rack aside and grabbed the metal latch on the top of the trapdoor, pulling it open. Four wooden steps led them down into a basement which ran under the whole house.

'Shall I pull the trapdoor closed?'

Freda nodded. 'Of course, if our house is bombed we could be trapped down here and they might not think to look for us.' Her tone was matter of fact.

'Feeling positive, are we?' Both women smiled at the irony of the situation; a choice between being stuck underground or being buried below a pile of rubble.

There was enough head room for the women to stand unimpeded. A narrow, rectangular window at street level cast a dull light; enough to break the darkness but not enough to lift the gloom.

'What will you do now the Scouts hut is destroyed?' Freda had perched on a small wooden stool, offering her friend the only chair.

'Look for the next best thing, I suppose. But with more children to teach, finding a big enough classroom is proving a challenge. Although to be honest with you there's not much teaching going on most days.'

There was no way of knowing exactly where the bomb had landed at that moment, but both women knew it was close by. Close enough to make the foundations of the house shake and the glass in the little window shatter. They held hands, gripping each other tightly, waiting for the shaking to subside. It wasn't just the house that was shaking. Each experience was as bad as the first; the apprehension building from the moment the sirens sounded, the terror of the blast, followed by the fear of who might have been hurt, or worse still, killed.

'Too close for comfort that time,' Freda said, moving towards the broken window. 'I can't see anything from here.'

'Come away from there. If there's another one...' Phyllis pulled her friend back. 'We'll wait for the all clear then we can go up and find out the worst.'

Neither of them counted the minutes as they sat holding hands and waited. It wasn't a time for conversation, each was absorbed in her thoughts. After the thunderous noise of the bomb blast the silence was almost eerie. Then the sound of footsteps, but it was difficult to tell if the sound came from outside, or from right above them. At last the siren announced the all clear. It was only then that both women realised they had been holding their breath.

Freda was the first to move forward towards the trapdoor. 'Come on, let's get back upstairs. We deserve a cup of strong hot tea.'

Standing on the top step she pushed at the door. 'I can't budge it.' The fear in her voice was thinly disguised.

'Here, let me try.' Phyllis gently eased her friend to one side. Steadying herself on the step, with her feet as wide apart as possible, she gave a forceful shove to the trapdoor, but there was no moving it.

'What about if we both try at the same time?'

'There's barely space for us both to stand on the top step.'

With a little negotiation they managed to reposition themselves so they could simultaneously put their weight behind one big push. Still the trapdoor would not give way.

'What time is your Arthur due home?'

'ARP wardens don't exactly keep regular hours. He'll come home when he's done all he can to help whoever needs helping.'

'Well, right now I'd say that's us.'

'Yes, but he doesn't know that, does he?' The frustration of the situation, mingled with fear, was inevitably leading to irritability.

'We could call out of the window, someone's bound to hear us.' Phyllis's spirits lifted as soon as she voiced her plan.

Freda was the first at the window. It was dusk now, with barely any light filtering into the basement. They listened, detecting the sound of a fire engine in the distance. There were several voices too, someone shouting but the words weren't clear enough for them to distinguish what they were saying. Freda put her face as close to the broken window as possible.

'Help,' she shouted, taking a deep breath and then again, 'Help.'

'Two voices will be better than one. Ready, I'll count to

three.'

After several attempts with no response from outside they paused.

'Did you hear that?' Phyllis said.

'What?'

'Something above us. Footsteps.'

'Let's bang on the hatch. If someone is in the house they'll hear us.'

They moved quickly back to the wooden steps. Phyllis removed one of her shoes and banged it repeatedly on the underside of the trapdoor.

'We're down here,' Freda shouted, 'in the basement.'

'Freda.' Both women recognised the voice of their rescuer.

'Arthur, thank goodness. The trapdoor is stuck, we can't open it.' Freda had barely finished her sentence when the hatch opened, revealing her husband's face. 'I thought when I walked down the aisle on our wedding day and saw you standing there it was the best moment of my life, but I think this has just beaten it.'

'That old shoe rack had fallen across the trapdoor. It must have tipped over when the bombing shook the place,' he told his wife, as the two women emerged from the gloom.

With the kettle on the gas, Phyllis was keen to know where the bomb had landed. 'It sounded so close.' Her own house was just at the end of the street, perhaps she would have nowhere to return to. A picture flashed through her mind of all her belongings strewn across the road, her clothes, her furniture, the keepsakes that reminded her of her dear mother. 'The hospital is safe, is it?' No amount of possessions would sustain her if anything had happened to Audrey.

'It took out Wilson's Outfitters and the whole front of Marley's Butchers. The place is in a dreadful mess. I need to get straight back to help with the clearing.'

'What made you come back here?' Freda knew the answer; the two of them were connected by an invisible thread.

Arthur kissed his wife on her cheek. 'I must go love.'

When the two women returned to the sitting room to resume their needlework, their thoughts were elsewhere.

'You'll want to get home to Audrey,' Freda said, not looking at her friend as she spoke. Instead she picked up a dark grey woollen coat that was on the top of the material pile. 'Look at this, I don't remember seeing this earlier, but it will make a beautiful skirt. I might even get a little waistcoat out of the top part. What do you think?'

'I'll go via the hospital, I told Audrey to wait there for me. She's too young to be wandering around on her own in the blackout. Although the truth is I'm more nervous than she is. She has nerves of steel that girl. Are you sure you'll be okay if I leave now?'

'You go on. I'll be just fine.'

Freda collected the empty tea cups and took them out to the kitchen. Phyllis had just put her coat on and picked up her sewing basket, when there was a knock on the front door.

'I'll go, if you like,' she called out to her friend.

The rap on the front door was urgent and business-like, making her heart thump uncomfortably in her chest. It had been a challenging few hours and she would be pleased to be home safely with her daughter. But her heart rate only increased when she opened the door to see a policeman standing on Freda's doorstep. Her first thoughts went to Audrey. Although it made no sense that a policeman should be coming with news to Freda's house about something that may or may not have happened to Phyllis's daughter. But then nothing about wartime made sense.

'Mrs Latimer at home?' the policeman said. A formal approach was appropriate, even though he had known these people all his life.

'Freda is…'

Before she could finish her sentence Freda was behind her.

'Sgt Snow, what is it? It's not my Arthur, is it? He was here just a little while ago.'

Phyllis took her friend's hand, trying to convey strength in case the policeman had arrived with the very worst news.

'May I come in?' The policeman stepped forward without waiting for an invitation.

The two women followed the policeman along the hallway and into the sitting room. It was as though he had taken charge and they were happy to let him.

'It's not bad news, is it, Peter? You best just come straight out with it.' Freda clung to her friend's hand so tight that Phyllis was starting to lose the feeling in her fingers.

Sgt Snow looked around the sitting room and Phyllis and Freda followed his gaze. Then he moved towards the pile of clothes that lay across one of the chairs.

'What's this then?' he said, holding up the coat that Freda had been looking at just a few minutes earlier.

'A winter coat.'

'And where did you get it?'

'I'm sorry, I don't follow you.' Freda felt as though she had fallen into a radio drama where everyone was speaking a foreign language.

'Straightforward question, Mrs Latimer. When did you

take possession of this coat?'

'People donate clothes. You'll know all about that, I'm sure. It's to help those who are struggling, those in need.'

'That's one way of looking at it, I suppose.' Sgt Scott was still holding the coat aloft.

'Peter, you're not making any sense.'

'I am here in my official capacity, Christian names are not appropriate.'

'Official, in what way official.'

'Looting. A gentleman's outfitters is bombed. Clothes go missing. Clothes appear in a house not too far away and I ask myself, how did they get here? Got an explanation for me, have you?'

2
Audrey Frobisher

On the day she finished school Audrey Frobisher had one goal. Her focus had been the same throughout that last year at school - ever since war had been declared. As soon as she was eighteen she would join the Women's Auxiliary Air Force. Her ultimate dream was to be a fighter pilot, to seek retribution for all that was happening to the people around her. Over the last year she knew that soldiers from Tamarisk Bay had lost their lives. Someone had to pay.

Although her eighteenth birthday was four years away and surely the war would be over by then. Meantime her mother suggested she visit St Richard's Hospital, responding to their appeal for volunteers.

'I'm not cleaning up sick,' she told her mother. 'If that's what they ask me to do, I'll just say no.'

Phyllis was used to her daughter's fervour. Neither was she surprised when the bluster blew itself out on the first day she spent at St Richard's.

Over an early supper Audrey reported the events of the day. 'They asked me if I liked writing,' she said, still a little mystified at how the visit had turned out.

'Records take time to complete, I suppose. And with the nurses being so busy…'

'No, not records. Letters.'

'Letters?'

'Yes, the wounded soldiers need help to write to their loved ones. Some of them have their hands bandaged, others have lost sight in one eye, or both…' her voice tailed off as her memory of the some of the patients loomed large in her mind.

'And you'll be helping them?'

'Yes, listening carefully to their words and writing them down.'

'Quite a responsibility. I'm proud of you, Audrey. With you to talk to they won't feel so alone.'

Audrey would never have admitted that the first time she walked into the ward and saw the wounded men, she felt daunted. It was one thing imagining the heroics of a conflict that was happening far away, but to see the results of shrapnel wounds, gunshot and gas attacks, made her stomach churn. She wondered if she might be better volunteering to work in the laundry instead. Never had the thought of ironing and folding seemed so attractive.

But then she sat beside the bed of a young soldier who may have been just four or five years older than her. His eyes were bandaged. She gave a little cough to alert him she was there.

'I'm Audrey,' she said in a whisper, in case he was sleeping.

His immediate reaction was to move one arm from under the bedclothes, easing his hand across the sheet, searching for contact. If a boy had done the same thing at school she would have given him a slap. But this boy had become a man the day he donned his uniform. He wasn't after a quick thrill, a thoughtless grope. He wanted to know he wasn't alone. Audrey laid her hand over his, 'What's your name?'

'John.'

It wasn't just John who she could help during her hospital visits. There was Matthew and Fred and Tommy. So many, each with their own stories, their own fears and sadnesses. Others would find their way to the laundry; it was here that Audrey could make a difference and here where she would stay.

Maybe young girls in Germany were doing the same thing. After all, German men who were losing their lives were no different to the British soldiers. They all had parents, loved ones, friends.

Over the days and weeks that followed Phyllis listened while her daughter recounted what she had been told and what she had seen. She had to suppress her motherly instincts, her desperate need to save her daughter from the reality of the conflict, the bloodshed. But there was no getting away from it, it was all around. Milward Road had been decimated just a week ago, with a mother killed, leaving behind a motherless child. Her three-year-old son had been playing out in the back yard and a high wall had sheltered the boy from the blast. Each family in Tamarisk Bay was affected; if it wasn't a relative who had suffered, it would be a friend, a neighbour, no-one was immune to tragedy.

So it was that earlier on that Thursday, before Phyllis went off to Freda's house, she was in her own kitchen, chatting to Audrey and preparing for another early supper.

'Let's take out that last flowerbed this weekend. It'll give us more space for potatoes,' Phyllis handed her daughter the chopping board. 'I'll peel, you chop.'

'It's a goat we need, not more potatoes.'

'A goat?'

'Yes, I miss cheese and I'm fed up with standing in a queue for ages just to pick up our pathetic rations. It's barely a mouthful.'

'Well, there's no chance of a goat. Anyway, if we did have one it would probably end up eating everything we are trying to grow.' Phyllis ignored the face her daughter pulled, which would have made any goat's milk turn sour. 'I'm going to Freda's straight after tea.'

'More sewing?'

'There are plenty who have nothing to wear. The bombing destroys every single possession for some, clothes included. And before we know it winter will be here and what with the coal rations…'

'We'll be wearing so many layers we won't be able to move. Which reminds me, mother, I think I've got a chilblain.'

'Will you come with me to Freda's? Your sewing isn't perfect, but you'll be a useful pair of hands.'

'I hate sewing.'

'I don't want you here alone. I'd rather you came with me.' Phyllis knew her daughter well enough to know that issuing an instruction would inevitably meet with refusal. Gentle cajoling was usually more successful.

'I'll go to the hospital.'

'In the evening? They won't want you there at this time of day.'

'Visiting hours. And most of those poor men have no-one to visit them. I'll be more use there than sewing buttons on or unpicking hems.'

So when Freda and Phyllis retreated into the basement that Thursday evening and when the bomb dropped, it was a consolation to Phyllis that her daughter was safe. Assuming, of course, that the hospital hadn't been bombed.

3
Thursday evening and Friday morning

With the house to herself again Freda sat in the sitting room staring at the fire. There were just enough coals to keep the flames alight, but she didn't see the flames, or the reddening of the coals. Her eyes were open, but her mind was focused on the events of the past few hours.
Sgt Snow had taken statements from her and Phyllis, after removing the offending coat, which he bagged as 'evidence'. Evidence of what, the two friends still didn't quite understand.

As soon as Freda had closed the front door behind the departing police officer, Phyllis grabbed her own coat from the coat stand in the hall. 'I must go and fetch Audrey. I told her to wait for me and I'm much later than planned. Will you be okay?'

'Why wouldn't I be?' Freda often resorted to a spikiness when things didn't go the way she wanted them to.

'Don't give the police a second thought. It's all nonsense. You'd think they'd have better things to do.'

Once Freda showed her friend out, she did just what Phyllis had advised her not to do. She gave more than a second thought to the unexpected police visit. She turned the evening's events over in her mind. If only she could recall where the coat had come from, who had donated it. People were generous with their hand-me-downs, but this was brand new and from the feel of it would have cost someone a packet.

Freda and Phyllis weren't the only ones to be heeding the government's advice of 'Make do and mend'. Clothes were needed for families who had lost everything in bombing raids and most of the children who had been evacuated from London down to the coast, arrived with nothing, bar a school satchel and a name tag. It wasn't just the sewing that occupied women all over Tamarisk Bay night after night. Anyone who had a moment to spare and an old woollen jumper or two to unravel would rework discarded items into gloves, socks, scarves, even balaclavas, many of which were collected and sent out to the men at the front.

One of the funniest stories Freda heard recently was from her neighbour, Eva. It seems that Eva had been collecting vegetable peelings to try to make enough dye to turn the wool from an old cream jumper into a nice red scarf and hat. Instead, all she'd succeeded in doing was to turn the cream into a ghastly puce. But puce or not it would still keep someone warm.

'Try tea leaves next time,' Freda told her neighbour, 'they work a treat and any kind of brown has to be better than that puce. Besides, the vegetable peelings would make a good soup, seems a waste to use them for dye.'

Each person had their own opinion about what was wasteful.

Freda stared into the fire for at least another hour and then Arthur finally arrived home. Hearing the back door open shook her out of her reverie. She joined him in the kitchen.

'Take those clothes off and give them to me,' she told him. 'I can barely see your face, it's thick with…soot is it, or brick dirt?'

'Bit of everything. The whole of Bridge Street, it's such a mess Freda, it'll take ages to clear it properly.'

'You've done what you can. Sit there and I'll make you something to eat.'

'Just a cup of tea. I've got no appetite after what I've seen.'

'Who got it this time? No, don't tell me.'

Arthur shook his head. Since he first started as an Air Raid Precautions Warden he had vowed not to talk to Freda about his work. 'Let's keep our life inside these walls as normal as we can,' he'd told her. In truth he knew that over the weeks and months to follow he would see sights that would keep him awake most nights. Describing them to Freda would only serve to make them even more real. She'd see for herself soon enough.

'At least have a sandwich, you've not eaten since this morning.'

'Are you okay?'

'Me?'

'Being stuck down in the basement can't have been much fun. Must have given you a scare.'

'What made you come back?'

'Once the all clear sounded I told the others I'd have to check on you, make sure you were okay.'

'Just as well. Poor Phyllis was so worried about Audrey. I've said nothing up to now, but I can't help thinking that it's not right, a young girl getting mixed up with wounded soldiers.'

'Mixed up how?'

'Oh, take no notice of me. I'm just a bit out of sorts.'

They sipped their tea in silence. Freda tossed the options around in her mind. She would have to tell Arthur about the police visit, but it would make little difference if she waited until the morning. At least then her husband might have the chance for a few hours sleep. It wasn't as though he could go to the police station tonight, despite Sgt Snow's insistence to the contrary.

She could tell from the haunted look in her husband's eyes that someone had died in the bomb blast. Maybe more than one person. He'd had more than enough to deal with for one day.

'Another cuppa?' She poured more hot water into the teapot and stirred it around, knowing there would be little strength left in the tea leaves.

Arthur shook his head. 'I think I'll just sit here for a bit, enjoy the last of the warmth from the fire.'

'Don't dwell on it. You'll have done your best.'

'You go up, I won't be long.'

There wasn't much sleep to be had in the Latimer household that night. Before it was light Freda was down in the kitchen, filling the kettle and putting it on the hob. She knew Arthur would want to be off and out early to continue with the clearing and she had to tell him before he left.

She heard him padding around upstairs and poured his tea, then put a loaf and some butter onto the table.

'Sit yourself down, drink your tea and don't get upset,' she said, as soon as he came into the kitchen.

Arthur yawned and looked at his wife. His body was awake but his mind was still struggling to raise itself from slumber. 'I don't mind there's no jam. A buttered slice will do me fine.'

'I'm not talking about jam. I need to tell you something and it'll make you riled, but you're to stay calm. We'll sort it out between us.'

He sat, sipping his tea, waiting for his wife to continue.

'The police came here last evening.'

He looked at her through eyes still bleary with sleep. She carried on, keeping her voice calm and smooth. 'They wanted to know about a coat.'

'A coat?'

For now, echoing his wife was the most he could manage.

'A coat turned up on our needlework pile and Peter Snow took it away.'

'Are the police suddenly desperate for a supplement to their uniform?' Arthur's attempt to lighten the mood was wasted.

His wife continued. 'They want to know how the coat came into my possession.'

'Folk are donating all the time. Freda, love, I need to be getting ready. There's so much to do today and I'll not leave it to others.'

'The thing is…they want to talk to you.' She poured the remains of her tea down the sink, turning away from her husband. She knew he would have a barrage of questions, none of which she could answer. She ran some water into the sink and, keeping her back to him, she explained the rest of the conversation she had had with the police officer the previous evening. Although, in truth, it had been more of a question and answer session than a conversation.

'And Phyllis?' Arthur said when she finished speaking.

'Yes, Phyllis was here, as you know.'

'Did they question her about the coat?'

'She knows as little about it as I do.'

Freda and Arthur walked together to the police station in silence. There was little Freda could do to soothe her husband's annoyance when she was just as angry.

'We're here to talk about a coat,' Arthur announced to the constable at the desk.

'A coat, sir?'

'Sgt Snow came to our house last night and removed a coat and we're here to talk about it.'

'And your address is?' The PC knew the importance of being thorough.

'23 Maple Avenue,' Freda used the sharpest tone she could. She remembered the young constable when he was still in short trousers.

The desk officer shuffled through the various notes spread out in front of him. 'If you could wait here please.'

They watched him disappear down the corridor, re-emerging moments later, followed by Sgt Snow.

'Mr and Mrs Latimer, if you could follow me please.'

They may have all grown up together, exchanged marbles in the school playground, but now Peter Snow wore a police uniform, with all the formality that came with it. His deep forehead gave the impression he was always frowning, which in reality perhaps he was.

Once the three of them were seated in the interview room there was barely room to swing the proverbial cat. Sgt Snow sat first, kicking the wastepaper basket that someone had unhelpfully placed beneath the table. Cigarette ends spilled out onto the floor and Freda had to stop herself from bending to pick them up.

'Why are we here?' Arthur had no intention of hiding his disgust. 'I've got important work to do and so have you.'

The sergeant raised an eyebrow. 'Be very careful with your tone. Remember you are talking to an officer of the law.'

'And you are talking to someone who spent last night dealing with real loss and I'm not just talking about buildings.'

'And that is exactly why you are here.'

'Because I'm helping folk put their lives in order?'

'Because it appears it's not just the bomb damage that's being cleared.'

Freda watched the expression of the two men. The sergeant's eyes narrowed and her husband's face reddened as his blood pressure rose.

It was half an hour later before Freda and Arthur emerged from the police station. Sgt Snow had presented the coat to them in a determined fashion, announcing that Wilson's Outfitters had confirmed it was one of theirs. Arthur said little while his wife demanded an explanation as to why they were being questioned.

'An ARP warden was seen removing the coat, along with several other items,' Sgt Snow announced.

As Freda listened to the sergeant explain the likely sequence of events, she thought through all she remembered about the previous evening. She had heard footsteps, but then Arthur had released them from the basement, so the footsteps must have been his. Could someone else have brought the coat just before Arthur arrived? Who would have done that, and why?

Standing outside the police station she shared her thoughts with her husband, but Arthur was so intent on getting back to work she could tell he was barely listening.

'I can't think about that now. And neither should Peter Snow be thinking about it. There's real criminals to be caught, real crime to deal with.'

'You heard what he said, looting is becoming a real problem. They need to nip it in the bud.'

'They can nip what they like, as long as they leave us out of it.'

'I'll call round and speak to Phyllis, see what she thinks.'

As Arthur walked away she called after him. 'Ask the other chaps who were there yesterday, see what they remember.'

A shrug of his shoulder was her only reply, although she hadn't expected anything else.

4
Friday, 6th September 1940

While Sgt Snow was interviewing Freda and Arthur, Audrey was conducting enquiries of a different kind.

She arrived at St Richard's so early that the Ward Sister told her she would have to wait in the corridor for at least an hour while the men had their early morning wash and breakfast. She took the opportunity to make a few notes in her journal.

As part of her induction to the hospital volunteering they had explained that she should spend no longer than half an hour with each patient, to show no favouritism. But whenever the nurses left the ward she returned to John's bedside. It was nothing to do with his looks; after all most of his face was bandaged. Yes, he was one of the younger patients, but then Charlie Roper in Bed 6 was similar in age. It was more that John had a knack of making her laugh, which was quite something when he'd been told there was a possibility he would lose his sight.

'I'm supposed to be cheering you up,' she told him during her last visit.

'You do. Ever since you described the way Matron stands to attention every time Dr Taylor enters the ward, I have the perfect picture in my mind. I have to stop myself smiling. In fact the other day she asked me what I had to laugh about and I had to pretend to have hiccups.'

Audrey had never expected her hospital volunteering to involve such joviality. As she sat in the corridor, waiting for the nod from the Ward Sister that the patients were ready, she had to suppress a giggle.

When she did enter the ward her eyes were immediately drawn to John's bed, only to see it was empty. A combination of her stomach turning over and an uncomfortably fast heart beat made her feel quite queasy.

'Excuse me.' She approached one of the nurses who was clearing away the last of the breakfast things. 'Jonathan Larch? He's not been discharged, has he?'

The nurse hesitated for a moment and in that moment Audrey formed pictures in her mind of standing by a graveside holding a single rose. She shook her head and realised she had missed the nurse's reply.

'Pardon?'

'He's been wheeled round to see the eye specialist, Mr Whitfield. He's got his own office on the other side of the hospital. You're one of the Girl Guide volunteers, aren't you?'

Audrey nodded.

'William Harris, Bed 4. He could do with some cheering up. He's been told it'll be another week before he can be discharged. The wound on his leg isn't healing as quickly as we'd like.'

William Harris appeared to be sleeping, but as soon as Audrey approached his bed he opened his eyes, startling her a little. He was around the same age as her dad, but everything else about him reminded her of a prize fighter; reddened cheeks, a bulbous nose and fingers like thick sausages.

'Hello, I'm Audrey.'

He peered at her, his expression a mixture of mistrust and disdain.

'And what does Miss Audrey think she's doing sitting beside my bed?'

'I've…' What was she doing? The last time she felt so insignificant, so childish, was in her first year at school when Tommy Bevans pushed her over in the playground.

'You'd rather be mooning over young John Larch.' His gruff voice matched his demeanour.

'I'm sorry?'

'I've been watching you. Creeping over to his bedside every time the Ward Sister isn't looking. Be careful, girly.'

'Why would I need to be careful?'

'The apple never falls far from the tree.'

For a bullish man he seemed to have plenty of flowery words.

'Told you about his dad, has he?'

Several uncharitable thoughts crossed Audrey's mind, all the very antithesis of what she was supposed to be doing here in the hospital.

'I understand your discharge from hospital might be delayed? Did you want me to write to anyone for you? To let them know how you are?'

It was only when she heard William Harris laugh that she realised laughter could be cruel.

'I can write my own letters. Not that my missus will be too interested. She'll have some fancy man keeping her warm at night, if I know my Jeannie.'

Audrey blushed despite herself and turned her face away and in doing so she saw the moment when John re-entered the ward, his wheelchair being pushed by an orderly. She could see that the bandages were gone from his face, but that's all she could see. Had his sight been restored? She couldn't tell from where she was standing and she couldn't risk getting any closer. She had to get out of the ward before John saw her.

'Keen to get back to him now, I expect?' William said, causing her to turn back to him. 'Just don't be taken in by him, that's all I'm saying. You seem like a nice enough lass.'

She rehearsed her reply silently before opening her mouth. All the things she wanted to say, such as 'Mind your own business' or 'What makes you think you know me,' would all have got her kicked out of the hospital for insolence. Instead she said, 'Is there anything I can do for you before I leave?' She forced a smile, which came out like a grimace.

'Just ask him about his father,' William said and with that he closed his eyes. She had been dismissed.

Phyllis was ironing when Freda arrived and was pleased for a reason to stop. With tea made and the fire stoked up with a few more coals, Freda recounted the events at the police station.

'Why won't Peter Snow tell you why Arthur is a suspect? Is there a witness? If it's anyone in Tamarisk Bay, then we'll know them. I'll be round their house in a jiffy, giving them a piece of my mind.'

'It'll be a straightforward case of someone getting hold of the wrong end of the stick. I expect they saw Arthur helping to clear away the debris.'

'That's all well and good, but why accuse him of stealing? It doesn't make sense.'

'Nothing the police do makes sense to me. They complain they're short of manpower, with all the men off fighting and they waste time chasing the theft of one winter coat.'

'That's just it though, as far as we know it's not stolen at all. If we can work out who donated it then Arthur is off the hook.'

'You're talking as though we need to give him an alibi. My Arthur has done nothing wrong. He spends his days and even some of his nights trying to help folk and this is the thanks he gets for it.'

The warmth from the fire was comforting, but not enough to cause Freda's face to flush as red as a poppy.

'I'll pour us some more tea.'

At the very moment Phyllis went to fill the kettle, the back door flung open and Audrey stomped in, taking both women by surprise. Before Phyllis could say a word, her daughter pushed past her and ran upstairs to her bedroom.

'Oh,' said Freda. 'Looks as though someone's lost a shilling and found a sixpence. Had you best go to her?'

Phyllis shook her head. 'Teenage girls are best left alone when they've got their sulky face on. Or so I've come to discover.'

Once in her bedroom Audrey paced around, stopping occasionally to look at herself in the dressing table mirror. During the walk back from the hospital her only thoughts were that she was much too young to catch John's attention. She was also much too plain. She didn't have the high cheek bones and neat nose that her favourite film stars had, or the porcelain skin. In fact, much to her horror, in recent months she'd suffered two bouts of acne, which spread all over her forehead and chin. She kept her fringe brushed forward in a vain attempt to hid the angry pimples on her forehead, but there was nothing she could do to cover the blemishes on her chin. And now John had had his bandages removed he would see all her faults. For one fleeting moment a thought crossed her mind that it might be better if he didn't regain his sight. She could remain a mysterious voice, like an actress on the radio, with no fear of criticism over the clothes she wore or her looks. But since she'd had that thought she had been weighed down with guilt.

It was only when she stretched out on her bed, staring up at the ceiling, that she recalled what William Harris had said. Just as likely to be the jealous ramblings of an old man.

And yet…the first time she'd helped John write a letter she'd asked him how he wanted to start it. 'Dear mum and dad, or mother and father?'

'Dear mum,' he'd said, with a hint of something in his voice. Something she couldn't quite place. At the time she'd reprimanded herself for not being more aware; of course, his father would be fighting, maybe even injured, or worse. It wasn't her place to push him and John never offered to explain. From then on, during each visit, he would dictate long letters to his mother. Audrey was fascinated with how he had so much to say, despite laying for weeks in a hospital bed and before that seeing the worst of a horrible war.

His letters said nothing of the fighting, or of the pain and frustration he must have felt at not being able to see. Instead, he asked his mother to share all her news. He was keen to know how she was managing for food, now that rations had been cut, how she was coping with her job. Between John's questions and his mother's replies Audrey formed a picture. She learned that Mrs Larch helped to run a mobile bathing and laundry service in Brighton. She was one of a team of four who operated a lorry that was once used by the fire service. The vehicle had been converted into three compartments, with dressing rooms for five people at each end, with the shower-bath in the middle. The team set up near to schools, helping children to bathe under the supervision of their teachers.

Audrey was fascinated by the idea and described it to her mother, but Phyllis was so sceptical that such a thing was possible they ended up rowing about it. Audrey vowed never to tell her mother another thing.

She laid her head on the pillow and pulled her bedspread up over her feet, letting out a heavy sigh. There would be no more letters to write, or funny anecdotes to read out to John. She loved watching his face spread into a smile that made the bandages crinkle at the side of his head. If he could see again he would write his own letters, she was no longer needed.

'Can I come in?' Phyllis's voice outside the bedroom door brought Audrey back to the moment.

'No,' she said, not hiding the defiance in her voice. Her mother would want to know all the whys and wherefores and then she would make assumptions and they would all be wrong.

'I'm coming in anyway.'

Audrey muttered something under her breath, which Phyllis chose to ignore as she pulled a chair over next to her daughter's bed. 'Are you going to tell what's the matter?'

'Why should anything be the matter?'

'Have you looked in the mirror? A face like that tells me something is the matter.'

Audrey shrugged, pushed the bedspread away, swung her legs round and sat on the side of the bed. 'I'm thinking of helping out with the salvage scheme.'

'As well as the hospital visiting? You'll be busy, but good for you, if you're sure.'

'Instead of the hospital visiting. They don't need me anymore.'

Phyllis remembered her own adolescence well enough to recognise the signs. It was more than likely that her daughter had her heart set on a boy and something had happened to leave her disappointed. It would be Audrey's first experience of a broken heart, but her mother was certain it wouldn't be her last.

'Freda was here just now.' Talking about other people's woes was bound to be a safer subject. 'Arthur is having some trouble with the police.'

Audrey raised an eyebrow. 'Mr Latimer in trouble with the police? Well, there's something I never thought I'd hear.'

'The police have the wrong end of the stick, something about a coat that's gone missing from Wilson's Outfitters. But we need to do what we can to help sort it out.'

'We?'

'Freda and Arthur are our friends. Besides, I was there at Freda's when Sgt Snow called round. Just last night.'

'Ah. If it means we can prove Sgt Snow wrong then I'm all for it. I've never forgiven him for accusing me of shoplifting that day. Do you remember, mum? It was my sixth birthday. Mr Gage had given me a handful of toffees and Sgt Snow was convinced I'd pinched them.'

'It was just a misunderstanding. It does no good to harbour grudges. Sgt Snow is just trying to do his best to keep our community safe. It can't be easy with all that's going on.'

But Audrey's memory of her indignation eight years earlier only served to fuel her resolve.

'I'll ask about,' she said, grabbing a cardigan from the hook on the back of her bedroom door.

'Whatever you do, be polite and mind your manners.'

'Don't I always,' she said, giving her mum a hug before running out of her bedroom and moments later out of the house.

There were a couple of routes Audrey could take from her home to Bridge Street. The cut through from Warren Road to Bexley Avenue was almost completely blocked following a recent bombing raid so she chose the longer route, up past the Latimer's house and through the churchyard. She'd become used to seeing the aftermath of what appeared to be indiscriminate bombings in and around Tamarisk Bay. In these 'hit and run' raids the Germans dropped any bombs remaining from the London blitz before heading back over the Channel.

She'd been thinking that any day she would have to share her bedroom with an evacuee, but now it seemed that children were being sent off to the countryside. The coast was no longer a safe haven.

Emerging from the churchyard she had her first view of the devastation that used to be Bridge Street. Although the far end of the road had taken the worst of the hit, there was brick rubble, glass and timber debris strewn along the full length of the street. The air was still thick with dust; she could taste it.

Wilson's Outfitters was in the centre of a small row of shops that included Gage's Newsagents, Parry's cycle shop and Marley's Butchers. Just outside the butcher's a group of men were working together, attempting to lift several heavy timbers that had fallen across a delivery van. She stood for a while just watching, noticing several other individuals each picking through the various piles of debris. Perhaps they were searching for their own belongings, a few bits and pieces remaining from a home that was no more. She felt a tightening in her stomach when she realised they could be looking for people; dead bodies who would have laid there overnight, undiscovered.

'Hey,' a voice shook her back to the here and now. 'Give us a hand, will you?' Two women were trying to upend what looked like the remains of a sideboard. As Audrey moved to help, a man joined them and with each person taking one corner they succeeded in righting it. The one remaining door fell off its hinges and out spilled crockery, plates, cups, saucers, all tumbling out onto the street adding to the rest of the broken contents of someone's life.

'Thanks,' one of the women said. 'You're Audrey, aren't you? Phyllis's girl.'

The tight-knit community of Tamarisk Bay had been brought even closer as they combatted the changes that had come to the town since the outbreak of war. Audrey knew there wasn't much that could be kept secret, which was precisely what would help her to ferret out the truth about the coat.

'Mrs Marley.' The butcher's wife was usually standing behind the cash till waiting to take the money and the meat coupons, not here in her coat and scarf, picking over broken furniture.

'Your shop,' Audrey said, starting to absorb the implications of what she was seeing.

'Just the front of it gone. The blast shattered the glass.'

'And you? And Mr Marley? Is he alright?'

'He's shaken is all. We were both upstairs, closed up just half an hour before it hit, otherwise it would have been a different story.'

'Was anyone...' She couldn't say the words.

Mrs Marley shook her head. 'Best not to think about that now, lass. On your way to the hospital, are you?'

Audrey had never seen a dead body. Some of the hospital patients looked close to death; the ones who laid on their beds, motionless, unresponsive. There was nothing peaceful about the way they looked and there would be nothing peaceful about someone who met their end by a ceiling or wall falling on them. She didn't want to think about it. Her thoughts went to John. She'd been able to forget about him for at least an hour, but now he loomed large in her mind. She had never asked him if he'd seen anyone killed. She guessed he must have done. After all, that was the whole point of this stupid war, the military were either killing or avoiding being killed themselves.

'Don't come too close.' She didn't recognise the man who spoke to her. He issued the command before attempting to soften it with, 'We don't want you tripping over now, do we?' Audrey was certain that a few minutes earlier she had seen him bend down, pick something up from the rubble and put it in his pocket.

'I've come to speak to Mr Wilson,' she said, moving towards the group of people who were hard at work at the far end of the road. Mr Wilson's limp was making his task more difficult as he ferried armfuls of debris across to an empty wheelbarrow. Mrs Wilson was there, pushing another full wheelbarrow away. Audrey guessed it would be going to a piece of rough land that lay to the back of Bridge Street. Minutes later Mrs Wilson returned, exchanging her empty wheelbarrow with her husband's full one. Absorbed as she was with watching, she reminded herself it was Mr Wilson she was here to talk to. If he was the one who had accused Mr Latimer of stealing then how was it he was happy to work alongside him now. It was only then that Audrey realised Mr Latimer was missing. Instead of his usual place among the team of workers, he was nowhere to be seen.

'Where's Mr Latimer? He's not hurt, is he?' A brief image flashed through her mind, her sitting beside the hospital bedside as she comforted Mrs Latimer. She shook the thought away.

'We asked him to go home. He's not welcome here.' It was the stranger who spoke, his long, dark sideburns and heavy eyebrows making him look older than he might have been. He glared at her, while the rest of the workers turned to look at him. It was difficult to read the expression on their faces, but he seemed to have taken charge. They may have felt uncomfortable following his lead and yet it was as if they had agreed to do just that.

'What do you mean he's not welcome? He's the ARP warden, it's his job to help people.' Audrey raised herself to stand as tall has her five feet five inches would permit, taking a defiant stance.

'You'd best go home, Audrey, this is no place for you.' Mrs Wilson spoke this time, a clear instruction, issued with a soothing tone.

It wasn't so long ago when Audrey would have stamped her feet, displaying the truculence of a child. But her childhood days were over. She held the stare of the stranger until he was the one to look away. She wished she was brave enough to confront him about whatever it was he had put in his pocket. Instead she slowly turned and walked away from the group, sensing their eyes following her until she reached the end of the street.

Cutting through the churchyard again she made her way to the Latimer's house. Her mother would tell her not to interfere, but she was on a mission now, determined to ferret out the truth.

Freda opened the door to her with a look of hopeful anticipation on her face, which immediately faded to disappointment when she saw who was there on her doorstep.

'Audrey.' The statement offered no encouragement and it would appear no invitation to enter.

'Can I come in? Is Mr Latimer here? I need to speak with him.' She'd made no plans beyond knocking on the door. Whatever followed now would have to be made up as she went along.

Freda opened the door a little wider, stood back and gestured to Audrey to follow her through to the kitchen where Mr Latimer was sitting, nursing a mug of tea.

'It's not a good time for us just now, Audrey,' Freda said. 'There's not a problem with your mother, is there? Is she alright?'

'I've been to Bridge Street. You weren't there helping them clear the site.' She directed her statement at Arthur and then paused. He had been staring down at the cold tea, but now he raised his head and looked directly at her. 'That's no place for you. You'd best go home. Your mother will be worrying about you.'

'Why weren't you there?'

He admired her persistence. 'It's complicated.'

'Does it have something to do with a stolen coat?'

'Arthur is right,' Freda said. This isn't something for you to get mixed up with. You'd best go home. Tell your mother I'll come round and see her later.'

'Why do the police think you stole the coat?' She wasn't going to let it drop. Mr and Mrs Latimer were good people, they deserved better than this. 'Sgt Snow has got it wrong. It's not the first time he's jumped to conclusions.'

'Looks like we've got ourselves a useful ally.' Freda smiled and took a cup and saucer down from the dresser. She'd been ready to fight alone to prove her husband's innocence, but Phyllis's girl had a spark of courage that reminded Freda of herself at that age.

Over fresh cups of tea Freda explained in more detail about what had happened the evening before.

'But no-one is saying why they think he did it.'

'That coat turning up here is all the evidence they need,' Freda said.

'Someone else could have put it there.'

'That's what I told Sgt Snow. People are always making donations to our make do and mend pile.'

'No, that's not what I mean.' Audrey pushed her empty cup and saucer away and stood up. What she was about to say next needed impact. 'What if someone stole the coat and brought it here on purpose to implicate Mr Latimer?'

'But why? Arthur doesn't have a single enemy. There's no-one who would want to see him locked up for a crime he didn't commit.'

'Well, that's what we need to find out, isn't it?'

6
Tamarisk Bay Police Station

When the news was first announced there had been plenty of arguments. Opinion on the Government's decision to release prisoners was divided. Some complained that criminals should stay locked up until they had served their full sentence. Others disagreed, saying the men were more useful as soldiers, and anyway it was only the criminals whose misdemeanours were relatively minor who had been let out early. Murderers stayed locked up, that's if they hadn't already been hanged for their crime.

The two opposing sides would never reach a consensus and it remained the topic of conversation in pubs, on street corners and outside church after Mass on Sunday mornings. Families who were able to welcome home a loved one some weeks or months before their sentence was up made a show of celebrating. Others kept quiet, hoping the ex-con could slip back into the community unnoticed. Then there were the wives and children who would have preferred the man of the house to remain behind bars. Seemed that the police were more keen to punish burglars than wife beaters.

Sgt Snow had his own opinion about it all. The prisons needed emptying to make space. There was talk of bringing in the death penalty for looters. Maybe that was harsh, but something had to be done. Until now he'd been lucky, folk in Tamarisk Bay hadn't committed the kind of crimes he'd heard about from fellow police officers in some of the larger towns and cities, like Brighton and London. One report he'd read described how looters raided a well-to-do café after it was bombed, ferreting around among the dead, looking for expensive jewellery. Seems they even cut people's fingers off to get the rings. If that was the way crime was going maybe they should be threatened with hanging, or life in prison at least.

It was up to him to nip this kind of behaviour in the bud, before it got out of control. He was already having to deal with too many episodes of wilful damage and delinquent behaviour. No surprise really, now that the town was teeming with youngsters evacuated from London. Most of them weren't in school, so they had nothing better to do than look for a chance to get into trouble. Probably commonplace in the inner city ghettos, but he wasn't going to stand for it in his town.

Although he'd be the first to admit that the last couple of days had left him feeling uncomfortable. It was important to make an example of anyone who stepped over the line, but he'd known Arthur Latimer for years, in fact they were at school together. Like everyone else in Tamarisk Bay, he knew only too well how hard Arthur worked in his job as ARP warden. And then there was Freda. She'd taken on the role of County Evacuation Officer when no-one else was prepared to. It must be a thankless task, having to deal with snivelling children who didn't want to be here and families who were taking them in - another mouth to feed when they could barely cope with their own.

'Tea, sir?' PC Oliver's arrival with a mug in his hand broke his train of thought. 'Two sugars, that's right, sir?'

'I can't justify two sugars. We're on the same rations as everyone else. Just because we're officers of the law doesn't mean we can take liberties.'

The police constable put the mug down and retreated before any more telling off. Sgt Snow was clearly in a bad mood today, but then it seemed as though he was in a bad mood every day. And how much sugar he had in his tea was unlikely to sweeten his temperament.

'Bring me that coat,' Sgt Snow's voice boomed out along the corridor before PC Oliver had managed to take many paces away from his sour-faced boss.

'The coat, sir?'

'Imbecile. If I wanted a parrot I'd have gone to the pet shop.'

The police constable hadn't a clue what parrots had to do with anything, but now wasn't the time to ask. A few minutes later he returned with an evidence bag containing a woman's coat, which he had logged in last night.

Having dismissed the PC with a wave of his hand, Sgt Snow removed the coat from the evidence bag and laid it out on the table. It wasn't as though looking at the blessed thing again would give him any answers. Useful fingerprints would be a non-starter. All he knew was that the coat had disappeared the afternoon of the bombing and had turned up where he'd been told it would - in the Latimer household.

But what about the rest of the haul? Old Mr Wilson had told him that there was another winter coat that had gone missing, together with two men's jackets and a complete suit. Walking away with that lot in your arms would be nigh on impossible, even amid the confusion of an air raid. So, either Arthur had one or more accomplices, or someone else was the mastermind and the clothes had been spread around so as not to gain attention. He'd hoped that if he leaned hard on Arthur and Freda then one of them would talk. Perhaps they were both excellent liars, or perhaps they were telling the truth. They certainly had motive; Freda was forever asking for donations and it would make sense for

Arthur to be tempted. But would Arthur really have risked his good name and reputation?

Sgt Snow shook his head. He'd learned over the years in this job that people do all sorts in a moment of madness.

The witness had told him he'd seen Arthur Latimer enter Wilson's Outfitters through the smashed plate glass window, put the coat in an old sack and walk away. When Sgt Snow had asked the witness why he hadn't approached Arthur, he'd not really given him a satisfactory answer. Peter Snow opened his pocket book and looked over the notes he had made at the time.

'It's not my job to nick villains,' was the man's rather odd reply. In fact, the whole interview was odd. He'd thought so at the time, but he'd been so keen to follow up the lead that he'd thought no more of it.

Anthony Smith, 1a Old Town Cottages, Tidehaven, was the name and address the witness had given him. The police officer asked him why he was in Tamarisk Bay.

'Lending a hand,' was his reply.

The whole interview had been one of the less successful ones he'd had. He usually prided himself on asking just the right questions to get people to open up. If it wasn't for this blessed war, he would have had the chance for promotion by now. He'd make an excellent detective inspector, he was sure of it. But all that would have to wait until Hitler was finally beaten.

He sighed, put the coat back into its evidence bag and returned to his interview notes.

'You say you don't know Mr Latimer?' he had asked the witness.

'I live in Tidehaven.'

'I see. How long have you lived there?'

'I'm not the suspect, am I? I'm just doing my duty and reporting a theft.'

'And you clearly saw him take the coat?'

'I said so, didn't I?'

'I'm guessing there was quite a melee; the aftermath of a direct hit like that usually creates initial confusion, folk trying to grab their belongings, worrying to see who might have been hurt.'

'I saw him take the coat.'

'And it was definitely the ARP warden?'

'I told you. I recognised the uniform.'

'And how long did you say you've lived in Tidehaven?'

'I didn't.'

At this point Sgt Snow had lost his temper, demanded the man explain himself and as a result his one and only witness had left the police station. With reduced manpower there was no chance of having him followed and when he was finally able to send PC Oliver to the address to track the man down he discovered there was no 1a Old Town Cottages in Tidehaven. The address was a pure fabrication, and Peter Snow was beginning to think so was much of Mr Smith's accusation.

Once Anthony Smith (if that was even his real name) had left the police station Sgt Snow went straight to the bomb site in Bridge Street, hoping to speak to any of the others who had been working alongside Arthur Latimer to get their take on events. But by the time he got there, only old Mr Wilson was there, trying to make sense of his damaged shop, sorting the clothes into piles; those that were irrevocably damaged and those that he might just be able to salvage with a stiff brush and a steam clean. It was then that Mr Wilson told him about the total number of missing items.

But there was something else niggling away at the back of the policeman's mind. As he made his way to the Latimer house he replayed one final question he wished he had asked Anthony Smith. 'And so, Mr Smith, you say you recognised the uniform of the ARP warden, but did you see his face?'

7

The Horse and Groom

When the architect responsible for creating Tamarisk Bay decided to locate the town's first pub in the heart of the seaside resort, he was thinking of the building workers. The men who were toiling to create the first south coast resort of its kind for wealthy Londoners to 'take the waters' needed a chance to relax and ease their aches and pains with as many pints as their measly wages could stretch to.

That was back in 1829, but now, some one hundred years later the Horse and Groom offered the same solace to much the same kind of people. The difference now though was that the shortage of beer meant it didn't flow quite as freely.

The pub landlord looked forward to Friday nights almost as much as his regulars did. Since the war had taken hold, Gordon Hamilton had had to take the difficult decision to open up Friday, Saturday and Sunday nights only. There just wasn't enough beer to last a whole week. Even with these reduced opening hours he often found that his customers could get through a whole barrel in one night.

But fewer opening nights also meant Gordon had too much time on his hands. With four nights to fill, not to mention the days, he'd put himself forward as a volunteer fireman. Although he'd be the first to admit he dreaded having to deal with a real fire, one where folks were burned alive. Luckily, as a part-time volunteer, he was more likely to be kept busy watching out for fires that might start up when a bomb dropped, or clearing the mess that a fire left behind.

'Why on earth did you go and sign up for fire watching, if you're afeared of fire?' Molly had asked him the day he came back from filling out the forms.

She was the only person he'd shared his fears with. After thirty years of marriage there was nothing he hadn't shared with her.

At just short of sixteen stone, he might be afraid of burnt bodies, but he wasn't scared of swinging with a brisk left hook if any of his regulars got out of hand. Training at the local boxing ring every week as a teenager meant he knew how to handle himself, which was handy in the pub trade.

'Thought these strong arms would come in handy,' he'd told her, picking her up and spinning her around.

'Put me down, you daft thing.'

That was months back. Now, with Molly being ill most days, he'd had to tell them he wasn't available for fire watching after all.

He prepared to unlock the door. He knew there would be a queue outside and he could make a reasonable guess about who would be at the head of it. Mitch McDonald had been coming into the Horse and Groom since he was old enough to drink his first pint and probably even before that. Gordon's predecessor would have turned a blind eye to youngsters downing a glass of ale, providing they came in with their father and didn't make a nuisance of themselves.

When Gordon took over he didn't make too many changes; the locals liked things to stay the same and he wasn't about to upset them. Molly had her own ideas, of course, wanting to prettify the place, but a pub wasn't meant to be fancy, all the men wanted was to down a pint or two in congenial company, maybe have a game of shove ha'penny or dominoes. Gordon had found some old drawings of the place when it was a board and lodging house, as well as a pub. Framing the drawings and hanging them around the pub walls was the furthest he went to satisfy his wife's idea of sprucing things up.

The banging on the door brought his attention back to the moment. He checked his watch and drew the bolts back, to allow the heavy door to swing open.

'Evening lads.' They tumbled past him, patting him on the shoulder by way of a greeting.

Since he and Molly had never been blessed with children, his regulars were his family.

'Where's that lovely missus of yours then, Gordon? You know we'd rather watch her pull our pints than having to gaze at your ugly mug.' Mitch McDonald limped over to his regular bar stool and eased himself onto it, letting his crutches lean up against the bar. Gordon had heard the account from others so many times and each time the story got added to. But as he understood it, Mitch had lost a leg in the Battle of the Somme and received a medal for bravery as a result. But Mitch never spoke of it and everyone knew never to ask him.

'She's still not too special, to be honest.' Gordon poured pints for the men who were propping up the bar.

'Sorry to hear that. Nothing serious?'

The truth was Molly had not been right for a while. Gordon wanted to get the doctor to look at her but she refused. 'I don't want any fuss,' was all she kept telling him. But the night-time coughing was getting worse and if she didn't rally soon, then he'd call the doctor regardless.

The pub was filling out now, with the queue at the bar two deep. Another pair of hands to help out would be useful but he couldn't justify the wages and most of the customers were happy to wait.

The majority of the floor space was taken up with rough wooden tables and chairs where the older customers liked to sit, nursing their glass of milk stout. The rest hovered by the bar, keen to get their tankards refilled as soon as they'd emptied them.

An hour or so into the evening and the atmosphere had settled. Gordon moved between the tables, collecting empty glasses and listening into a few conversations. Inevitably most of the talk was about the recent spate of bombings.

'Have you seen the mess they've made of Bridge Street?' Wilfred was another old soldier who thought his efforts in the Great War would mean there would be no more fighting. 'You'd think the Jerries had got the hint the first time around, wouldn't you? If they think they're going to beat us this time with their bully boy antics, they can think again.'

'Just what this country needs, a good shake up. Well done, Hitler, is what I say.' The voice came from the other side of the pub and several people turned to look at the speaker. Gordon moved to the man's table to get a closer look. He wasn't a regular, in fact, he was certain he'd never seen him in the pub before. His swarthy features, long sideburns and bushy eyebrows made him distinctive enough to remember.

'Think it's okay for folk to be bombed out of their homes, do you?' Wilfred stood up, pushing his chair back with enough force that it bumped into the man sitting at the adjacent table.

'Steady on there.'

Several of the regulars stood up and Gordon could see how a disagreement fuelled by excess alcohol could quickly turn nasty.

'Settle down, lads. People have come in for a nice quiet drink. Best not to let tempers start flying.'

He made his way back behind the bar, keeping an eye on the stranger and an ear out for raised voices that spelled trouble. Checking his watch he moved out the back and unlocked the side entrance. Everyone knew that the local constabulary liked to slip in for a swift pint towards the end of the evening. They also knew Sgt Snow liked to keep a low profile, cycling over from the station and leaving his bike hidden in the neighbouring field. What they all failed to understand was why Peter Snow wanted to keep his drinking habits so secret.

'Say that again.' Wilfred's raised voice caught Gordon's attention. Wilfred had moved over to stand directly in front of the stranger, with a fist raised. 'You're not welcome here, why don't you sling your hook before I really lose my temper.'

The stranger was a few inches taller than Wilfred and looked as if he could handle himself if it came to a fight.

'Call yourself a tight-knit community? Look at you, you're all ready to believe the worst of someone you've known all your lives.'

The rest of the pub crowd had stopped speaking now and all eyes were on the stand-off between the stranger and Wilfred.

'What do you know about it? You don't even live round here. Why don't you crawl back under whatever stone you came from.'

'He's too scared to show his face, isn't he? I reckon that must mean he's guilty.'

'We're not interested in what you reckon, or anything else that comes out of your mouth for that matter. Arthur is one of us.'

Until that moment Arthur Latimer's name had not been mentioned in the pub. His tankard would stay empty until his name was cleared. A man like Arthur could never be a thief, but it didn't pay to take sides or get involved. Best to let the police do their job.

'You'll be visiting him in prison, then will you?' The stranger had the last word, just before Wilfred threw the first punch.

Molly's shouts from upstairs went unanswered as Gordon moved forward to break up the fist fight that threatened to destroy several chairs and too many glasses. At the same moment Sgt Snow pushed open the side door to be confronted by the scene. Forgetting about any chance of a quiet beer he pushed his way between Wilfred and the swarthy stranger, swiftly ducking to avoid a powerful left hook.

'That's enough. Any more and I'll arrest you both.'

Gordon began to pick up the chairs while the rest of the customers turned back to their drinks. They had seen nothing. No-one wanted to become embroiled in police interviews and witness statements.

The police sergeant pulled the stranger to one side, keeping a firm hand on his shoulder despite the man's protestations. 'Mr Smith. Twice in the space of two days.'

'I was just defending myself,' Anthony Smith said, a smirk on his face, challenging anyone to disagree.

'I'm not interested in who started it, but I am interested in your address. Seems you provided me with a false address yesterday. You'll know it's an offence to lie to the police.'

8
Anthony Smith

When Anthony first heard the rumours about his early release he didn't believe them. It was all his fellow prisoners could talk about, but the prison officers wouldn't confirm the gossip at first. Then, with just one week's notice, the prison governor announced that all prisoners who only had three months or fewer to serve would be released early. Whether they were hoping all the ex-cons would join up, or whether they wanted the space to fill the prisons with new criminals - who knew. Who cared. If Anthony could meet Hitler he would shake his hand.

He'd spent the whole of his time in prison protesting his innocence. The sentence had been overly harsh, but without money for fancy lawyers he never stood a chance. In the end, although it was the judge and jury who pronounced the guilty verdict, there was only one person to blame for his incarceration. There had only been one witness, but his testimony had convinced the lot of them. Now it was payback time.

On the day of his release his few paltry belongings were returned to him; a wallet with no money in it, just a photo of his wife and son and the clothes he'd been wearing on his arrest, which now hung off him as though they belonged to someone else. Prison food didn't exactly encourage a healthy appetite.

He might be a few pounds lighter but he could still handle himself. In every run-in he'd had with other prisoners he'd always come out on top. After the first few punch-ups they knew to keep well away. Anthony wasn't the sort to make friends.

There would be no-one waiting outside for him as he stepped through the prison gates. He'd only had one visit from his wife in all his time inside. She stayed barely ten minutes, announcing he wouldn't be seeing her again. She was moving and had no intention of telling him where. When he asked about his son she told him he'd joined the army.

'Will he visit before he goes off?'

'He's gone already. He wants nothing to do with you. And when you get out you'd do well to leave us both alone.'

That part of his life was over and good riddance. She'd fussed over the boy, made him soft. Better to have no son at all than a lily-livered one.

With no money and nowhere to stay, Anthony wasn't sure where to head to. He'd heard stories about the way life on the outside had changed since the outbreak of war. It seemed to him there were more opportunities than ever to make a bob or two. And if the authorities expected him to join up they could think again. He might look strong and fit, but if he needed to develop an ailment or two and convince a doctor he wasn't 'a well man', then that's what he'd do. He'd had enough of being bossed around during his time inside, now it was time for Anthony to call the shots.

For the first couple of nights he dossed down in an old shed on the outskirts of the town. He knew Tamarisk Bay well enough to remember the patch of ground that was divided into allotments. Some of the larger plots had a shed and, provided he kept out of the way during the day, he could creep in there at night undisturbed and be gone early morning.

The first time the air raid sirens went off, he wished he was back in prison again - just for a fleeting moment. Being out in the open made him feel vulnerable, not a feeling that sat well with Anthony; not a feeling he had felt before.

He was down on the seafront when the noise started. He watched as everyone around him moved in one direction. They were headed to safety, he was sure of that. He followed them into a surface shelter in Caves Road. A few of the faces were familiar, but he had no fear they would recognise him. Before his imprisonment he had lived on the outskirts of the town, never wanting to get embroiled in the community. Easier to keep a low profile when no-one knew you and easier to keep your business your own.

Inside the air-raid shelter few people spoke, some had their heads bowed in what appeared to be silent prayer. Waste of time, in Anthony's opinion. There was no point in hoping God would help you, more important to help yourself.

He scanned the faces of the twenty or so people around him, looking for the face of the one person he had made it his mission to track down. He would find him, he was certain of that. And when he did he would follow him, find out where he lived and then plan his retribution.

Over the next couple of days he mooched about Tamarisk Bay. Food was hard to come by, but he had mastered the sleight of hand that meant shoplifting a bread roll here and there didn't pose a problem.

It was on the third day after his release that he spotted him. Strutting about in his ARP uniform like he owned the town, with his supercilious attitude, making out he was better than the rest. Anthony smiled. He would take great pleasure in bringing Arthur Latimer down to size.

If Latimer hadn't been poking his nose in that day of the robbery, Anthony would have got away with it. He was certain of that.

He'd been casing the jewellery shop for weeks, he knew exactly when there would be plenty of cash in the till. No point stealing the jewellery, it would be too hard to move it on without questions being asked. But a jewellers meant a good load of weekly takings, better than a measly newsagents, which had been his original target.

He waited until ten-o-clock on that Friday evening. No-one would be around. Folk were either at home or in the pub. With the threat of war looming the authorities had issued a leaflet giving guidance about the importance of people blacking out their windows. They hadn't made it the law back then, but people had started to heed advice. As soon as night fell the streets were deserted, making it perfect for Anthony. He'd walked along Queens Street so many times during the day, rehearsing his steps. He knew every raised paving stone, every rubbish bin and postbox; he could probably do it blindfold.

He dressed himself head to toe in black, pulled a balaclava over his face and picked up his tool bag with all he'd need to force entry. He knew it would only take him a few minutes to take the lock apart; that was the best way, no noise, no fuss.

What he didn't bank on was Arthur bloody Latimer. Latimer had already taken on the duties of ARP warden and being the busy-body he was he took his job a little too seriously, knocking on doors, reminding people that once Britain was at war then even a sliver of light would be enough to warn the enemy.

As Anthony came out of the shop, with the money in his tool bag, he walked straight into Arthur. There was a scuffle, Arthur grabbed at Anthony, resulting in him pulling off his balaclava. It didn't take long for the police to track him down, put him in an identity parade and with Arthur bloody Latimer being such an upright citizen, no-one doubted his testimony. Now he could get his own back.

Anthony had worked out his plan. All he needed to do was to follow the warden and seize the moment. In the aftermath of a bombing Arthur would be kept busy. Anthony could steal something unnoticed. Then he'd take it round to the Latimer house. That was the hardest part of the plan, getting the goods into the house without anyone spotting him.

So on that Thursday evening, when all the stars aligned, Anthony Smith stood and watched and really couldn't believe his luck. Perhaps there was a God after all.

9
The aftermath

When Mr Latimer told Audrey about the day he caught a thief it all suddenly made sense. She had been so excited that she'd jumped up and inadvertently knocked the table, spilling everyone's tea.

'That's it then,' she announced. 'This man - what was his name?'

'Anthony Smith,' Freda confirmed.

'This Mr Smith has come out of prison and wants revenge. He's followed you, stolen the coat and planted it in your home and then gone off and told Sgt Snow that you are the thief.'

Arthur hadn't said much, which Audrey was disappointed about as she felt rather pleased with her powers of deduction.

'Shall we go and see Sgt Snow now and tell him?'

Neither Freda nor Arthur seemed too keen. 'Best leave it to us to sort it out,' they said in unison.

So Audrey returned home feeling quite deflated. There was only one thing that could cheer her and that would be to see John. But it was a risk. If there was any look of disdain in his eyes when he saw her face for the first time, then she would feel worse than she did now.

She took the gamble and it paid off. His sight had been completely restored and now that the bandages had been removed from his face all she could do was gaze at every inch of his face; the scar around his left eye, the dimple in his chin when he smiled. And it seemed as though his smile was broader than ever, as though he wasn't worried about her blemished skin, or her girlish looks. She was so intent on gazing at him that she forgot to ask him if he'd had another reply from his mother. When she did ask she wished she hadn't, as his face fell into a frown.

'She thinks my dad has been released.'

'Released?' As she asked the question several pieces of the jigsaw fell into place. 'He's been in prison?'

This was the reason for William Harris's nasty insinuations. John was the son of a convict.

'What was his crime?'

'He made thieving his career. That and being heavy-handed with my mother whenever he'd had one too many pints.'

Audrey didn't know what to say.

'It's why my mother moved to Brighton, to get away from him.'

'Have you seen him? Has he been to visit you in hospital?'

John shook his head. 'He wouldn't know I was here, thank God. I want nothing to do with him. Mum and I even changed our name to make sure we could be shot of him.'

'What was your name before?' She had a feeling she knew the answer before he said it. 'It was Smith, wasn't it?'

John listened as Audrey recounted recent events, explaining how she'd been helping to clear a friend's name and in doing so had probably seen John's father - the swarthy stranger who had spoken roughly to her in Bridge Street.

'Sounds just like the kind of evil thing he would do.'

'Your father needs locking up again. Let's hope Sgt Snow gets it right this time.'

Peter Snow wanted to get it right, but at that very moment he was no further forward in knowing what 'right' was.

Since the first time he had seen the witness something was nagging away at him. He spent some time digging through files in the basement of the police station. He'd tracked down the police file on Mr Anthony Smith and worked out exactly what was at the heart of his accusations. Sgt Snow had been on secondment to Brightport Police Station when Anthony Smith had been arrested and found guilty, but reading through the file, it was plain to see this was all about retribution. Anyone could see Arthur Latimer wasn't a thief and with only the word of an ex-con to go on any judge would throw the whole case out of court.

What's more, Sgt Snow was pretty certain that old Mr Wilson had been confused about just how many clothing items had gone missing that night. Chances were that it was just that one coat, the one he was now convinced that Anthony Smith had stolen and planted in the Latimer house in an attempt to frame Arthur. He just wished he could find some way of proving it, or at least proving something else that he could pin on Anthony Smith to justify throwing him back in prison, which was clearly where he belonged.

The fight in the Horse and Groom wasn't enough to charge him with, nor was the fact that he had given a false address. The courts were too busy with the rise in serious crime since the outbreak of war to have their time taken up with petty law-breaking.

All the sergeant could do was issue a severe warning to the ex-con, suggesting he moved as far away from Tamarisk Bay as possible. 'You're not welcome around here,' he told him.

'Don't worry, I've done what I came here to do,' was his only reply.

The loyalty in the Tamarisk Bay community may have wavered for a short time, but a week later at the Horse and Groom the regular crowd welcomed Arthur Latimer back into the fold. Gordon told him the first fill of his tankard was 'on the house'. If Anthony Smith had tried to steal Arthur's reputation he hadn't succeeded.

Despite his eyes being heavy with sleep and his stomach being full of beer, Arthur knew he wouldn't be able to rest. Peaceful slumber wouldn't be his again for a long time. Everything he had done over the last week he'd done with the best of intentions, hadn't he? Or maybe no real intention, just a moment of weakness. He had seized an opportunity, saw the coat laying there, thought of his wife and her endless attempts to make do.

Making do was all they'd been able to achieve even before the war had started. A constant challenge of coping without, food rationing, petrol rationing, little or no coal to keep the fires burning, even being starved of light since the official start of the blackout one year ago.

Instead all he'd done was lower himself to the thieving behaviour of his accuser. The man he'd been so proud to have caught red-handed had seized his chance of payback.

The only thing that saved Arthur was the lifetime he had spent doing good, right up until that Thursday one week ago when he committed a crime. A crime he would never be punished for, except for the punishment he would impose on himself, tonight and every night, as he lay staring at the ceiling while his wife slept soundly.

MORE SUSSEX CRIME

The *Sussex Crime* stories are centered around the fictional seaside town of Tamarisk Bay. To date there are three novels in the series, which are set in the late 1960s, with young librarian and amateur sleuth, Janie Juke, solving crimes and mysteries.

In this, the second novella/short story in the *Sussex Crime* series we meet some of the same folk who appear in the novels, but many years earlier. Still focusing on Tamarisk Bay, these novellas/short stories are set during the Second World War years. The first novella/short story is entitled, *Divided we Fall*, where we learn about the exploits of Janie's father, Philip, who is just a boy when the story unfolds.

Here, in *More than Ashes*, we meet schoolteacher Phyllis Frobisher, and her daughter Audrey. We meet these characters again in the *Sussex Crime* novels. Phyllis is a great support to Janie Juke, and Audrey's daughter, Libby is an investigative journalist with a taste for adventure, who enjoys racing around Tamarisk Bay with her friend, Janie Juke, looking for clues and helping to solve mysteries.

If you would like to read more about this whole cast of characters, then look out for the full-length novels in the series:

BOOK 1: THE TAPESTRY BAG
BOOK 2: LOST PROPERTY
BOOK 3: THE INVISIBLE CASE

PRAISE FOR THE SUSSEX CRIME SERIES

'This was a great find. A librarian turns to sleuthing in 1960s England. Janie Juke, an Agatha Christie enthusiast, is a very likeable protagonist. A real page turner. I've already bought the next book in the series… hoping there will be many more to come.'

'I got straight into the story … I really like the way the author depicted the 60s …I felt as if I was there!'

'Intriguing detective story with lovely period setting and interesting characters. I'm looking forward to seeing what Janie Juke solves next.'

'Loved every page and didn't want to put it down. Can't wait until the next one in the series.'

'Thoroughly enjoyable book. Kept me interested till the end. Looking forward to the next one.'

'The glimpses into WW2 are particularly good. Solid writing, great story, and Janie as a character is growing on me. I hope there are more in the series.'

ABOUT THE AUTHOR

Isabella rediscovered her love of writing fiction during two happy years working on and completing her MA in Professional Writing.

The setting for the Sussex Crime mystery series is based on the area where Isabella was born and lived most of her life. When she thinks of Tamarisk Bay she pictures her birthplace in St Leonards-on-Sea, East Sussex and its surroundings.

Aside from her love of words, Isabella has a love of all things caravan-like. She has enjoyed several years travelling in the UK and abroad. Now, Isabella and her husband run a small campsite in West Sussex.

Her faithful companion, Scottish terrier Hamish, is never far from her side.

Find out more about Isabella, her published books, as well as her forthcoming titles at: **www.isabellamuir.com** and follow Isabella on Twitter: **@SussexMysteries**

By the same author

SUSSEX CRIME MYSTERIES
BOOK 1: THE TAPESTRY BAG
BOOK 2: LOST PROPERTY
BOOK 3: THE INVISIBLE CASE

SUSSEX CRIME STORY 1: DIVIDED WE FALL

THE FORGOTTEN CHILDREN

IVORY VELLUM: A COLLECTION OF SHORT STORIES